For the children at the
Olds Elementary School
in Alberta, Canada.

HAPPY HONEY

HAPPY AND HONEY

HAPPY HONEY

HAPPY AND HONEY

written by Laura Godwin
pictures by Jane Chapman

Aladdin Paperbacks
New York London Toronto Sydney Singapore

First Aladdin Paperbacks edition September 2001

Aladdin Paperbacks
An imprint of Simon & Schuster
Children's Publishing Division
1230 Avenue of the Americas
New York, NY 10020

The text for this book was set in Century Schoolbook
The illustrations were rendered in acrylic.
Also available in a Margaret K. McElderry Books hardcover edition.
Manufactured in the United States of America
10

The Library of Congress has cataloged the hardcover edition as follows:
Godwin, Laura.
Happy and Honey / by Laura Godwin ; illustrated by Jane Chapman. p. cm.
Summary: Honey the cat is determined to play with Happy the dog,
even though he is trying to sleep.
ISBN-13: 978-0-689-83406-6 (hc.) [ISBN-10: 0-689-83406-3 (hc.)]
1212 LAK
[1. Dogs—Fiction. 2. Cats—Fiction. 3. Play—Fiction.]
I. Chapman, Jane, ill. II. Title. III. Series.
PZ7.G5438 Hap 2000 [E]—dc21 99-46923
ISBN-13: 978-0-689-84235-1 (Aladdin pbk.) [ISBN-10: 0-689-84235-X (Aladdin pbk.)]

Meet Honey.
Honey likes
to play.

Meet Happy.

Happy likes
to sleep.

Wake up, Happy!

Honey has a ball
for you.

Go away, Honey!

Wake up, Happy.
Honey has a toy
for you.

Go away, Honey!

Wake up, Happy!
Honey has a kiss
for you.

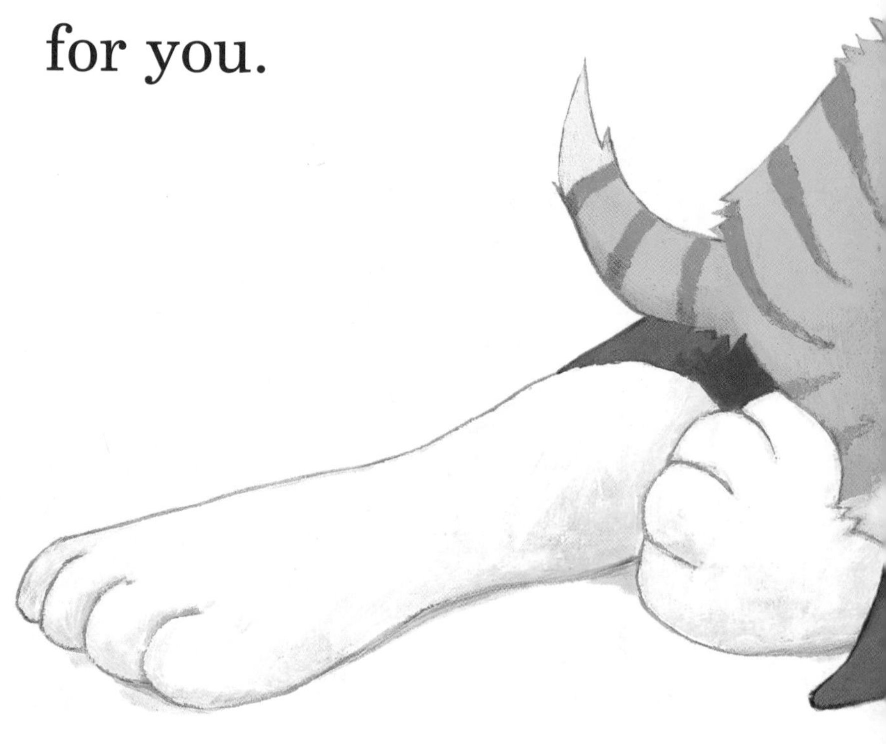

Go away, Honey!

Wake up, Happy!

Honey wants to
wash your tail.

Honey wants to
wash your ears.

Honey wants to
wash your nose.

Oh, oh! Happy wakes up.

Run, Honey, run!

Honey runs.

Oh, oh!
Happy runs.

Happy runs fast.

Honey jumps up.

Happy cannot
jump up.

Honey is happy.

Now Happy
will not sleep.

Honey will play
with Happy.

This is fun!

Happy Honey!